To David and Bakhta

This mini edition first published in 2008 by Andersen Press Ltd.
First published in Great Britain in 2008 by Andersen Press Ltd.,
20 Vauxhall Bridge Road, London SW1V 2SA.
Published in Australia by Random House Australia Pty.,
Level 3, 100 Pacific Highway, North Sydney, NSW 2060.
Copyright © Tony Ross, 2008
The rights of Tony Ross to be identified as the author and
illustrator of this work have been asserted by him in accordance
with the Copyright, Designs and Patents Act, 1988.
All rights reserved.
Colour separated in Switzerland by Photolitho AG, Zürich.
Printed and bound in Singapore by Tien Wah Press.

10   9   8   7   6   5   4   3   2   1

British Library Cataloguing in Publication Data available.

ISBN 978 1 84270 900 9

This paper is made from wood pulp from sustainable forests

# I Want TWO Birthdays!

## Tony Ross

Andersen Press
London

It was the Little Princess's birthday.
She had a royal cake and lots of presents.
"Mum," she asked, "why do you have TWO
birthdays, and I only have one?"

"Well," said the Queen, "queens always have two
birthdays. There's one for me to share with you,
and one to share with all the people."
"I want two birthdays then!" said the Little Princess.

So the Prime Minister put two birthdays in
the diary for the Little Princess.
One in the autumn, when she was born,
and one in the winter, to cheer things up.

Two birthdays meant two cakes and twice as many presents every year. "This is FUN!" said the Little Princess. "But THREE birthdays would be even better." So three birthdays were put into the diary . . .

. . . one in the autumn when she was born, one in the
winter to cheer things up, and one in the spring.
"Can't leave summer out," said the Little Princess.
"I want FOUR birthdays!"

The Little Princess loved her birthdays. She loved getting
up on the special day, and getting specially clean.
She loved the special cakes and all the special presents.

"Why can't I have MORE special birthdays?"
she thought.

So she had a word with the Prime Minister, and she had more birthdays put into the diary. Soon she had a birthday on every day of the year.

So every day, the Cook had to make another cake.
But they got smaller. And every day, everybody had
to buy presents. But they were not as nice.

The Admiral gave her a piece of chewing gum that he had finished chewing. The General gave her a piece of string with a knot in it. The Maid gave her a broken peg.

The next day, the King gave her a broken pencil.
"Tomorrow," he said, "you can have an old
pen with no ink in it."
"POO!" said the Little Princess. "These are rotten presents."

The Little Princess spat out that day's birthday cake.
"POO!" she said. "It's got no currants or anything in it!"
And last week's birthday cards were still on the mantelpiece

Every day, the Little Princess had to stay specially clean for her special birthday parties, but everyone stopped coming, because they couldn't afford the presents.

At last, Gilbert was the only one at the Little Princess's party.
"Where's my present, Gilbert?" she asked.
"Haven't got one, 'cos I'm only a toy bear," said Gilbert.
"Happy birthday!" At least, that's what she thought he said.

The very next day, the Maid came into the Princess's room. "Happy Birthday, Princess," she said. "Get up and get specially clean for your birthday. You've got another party, you know."

"Oh NO!" groaned the Little Princess. "Not again! Why can't I play like I used to? Why can't I get dirty?" "Because today is your BIRTHDAY," said the Maid. "Put on this nice clean crown."

"EVERY DAY is my birthday!" cried the Little Princess.
"I want a SPECIAL day, different to all the others."
"We must go and see your mum and dad then," said the Maid.

"I want a SPECIAL day, different to all the others!" said
the Little Princess.
"HMMM!" hmmmed the King. "What you need is an unbirthday,
just one unbirthday every year, and that will be your special day

"Wheee!" squealed the Little Princess. "Lovely, what day shall I have my unbirthday on?"
"How about the day you were born? We can all remember that, and it's next Wednesday."

The Little Princess was SO excited.
She had to wait a whole week until her
unbirthday arrived . . . and when it did arrive . . .

. . . the Cook baked a VERY special unbirthday cake
and everyone brought VERY special presents to the
unbirthday party. And the Little Princess had
a VERY special day.

And she had to wait a whole year until the next one!
"I wish I had an unbirthday every day!" she said.

"If you did, then it wouldn't be special, would it?" said the Maid.